SCOOBY-DOO! PICTURE CLUE BOOK

THE SHAMROCK SCARE

By Courtney Tyo

Illustrated by Duendes del Sur

Hello Reader — Level 1

P9-DMW-571

Visit Scholastic.com for information about our books and authors online!

ISBN 0-439-55715-1

12 11 10 9 8 7 6 5 4   4 5 6 7 8 9/0

Designed by Maria Stasavage
Printed in the U.S.A.
First printing, February 2004

SCHOLASTIC INC.

New York   Toronto   London   Auckland   Sydney
Mexico City   New Delhi   Hong Kong   Buenos Aires

It was St. Patrick's Day! 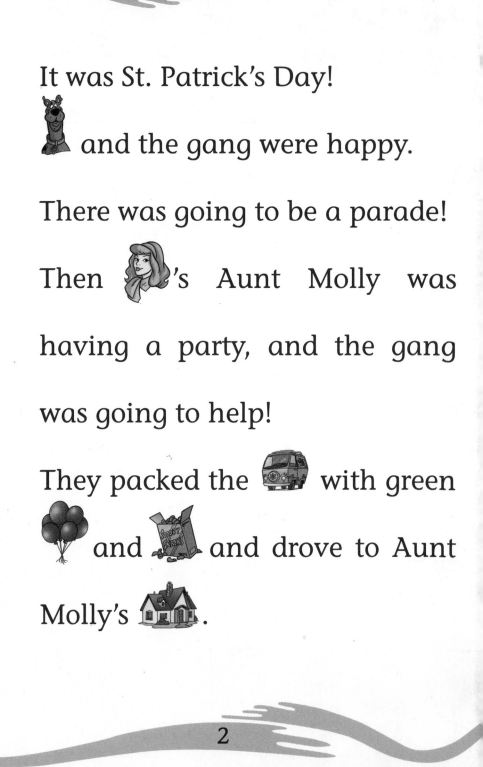 and the gang were happy.

There was going to be a parade! Then 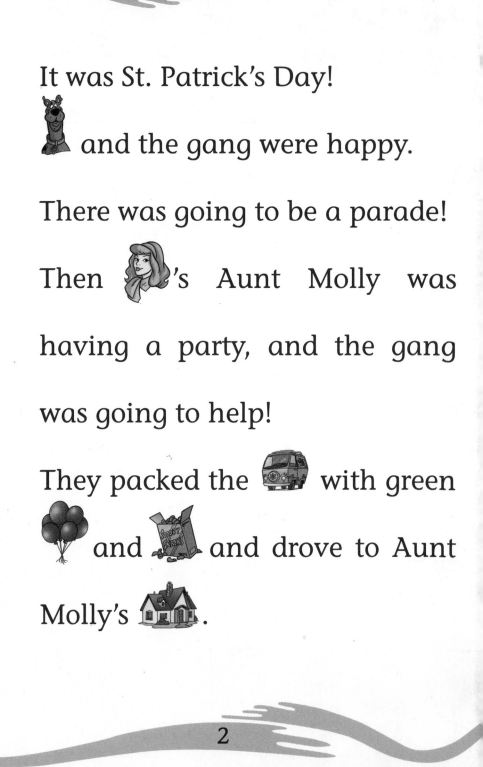's Aunt Molly was having a party, and the gang was going to help!

They packed the 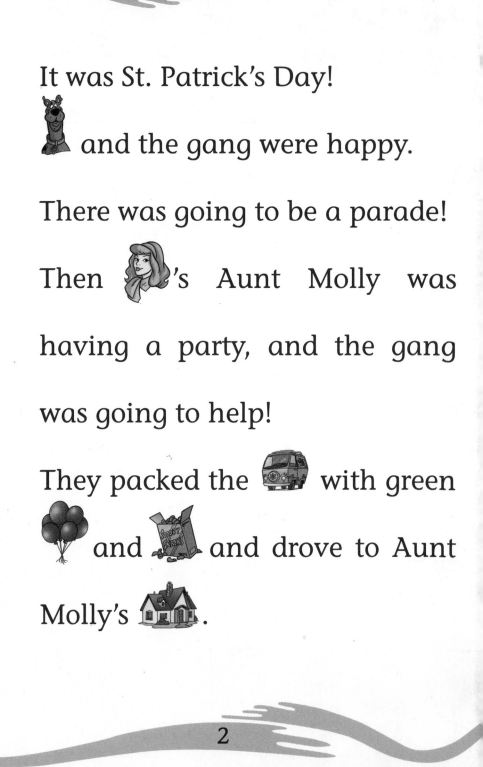 with green 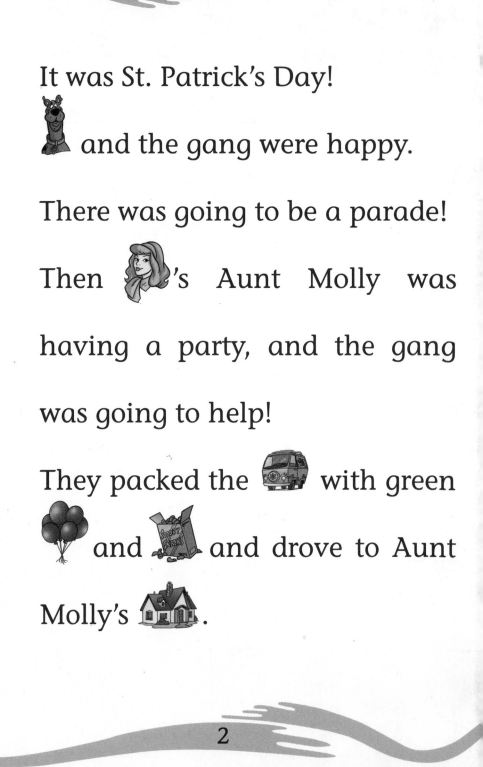 and 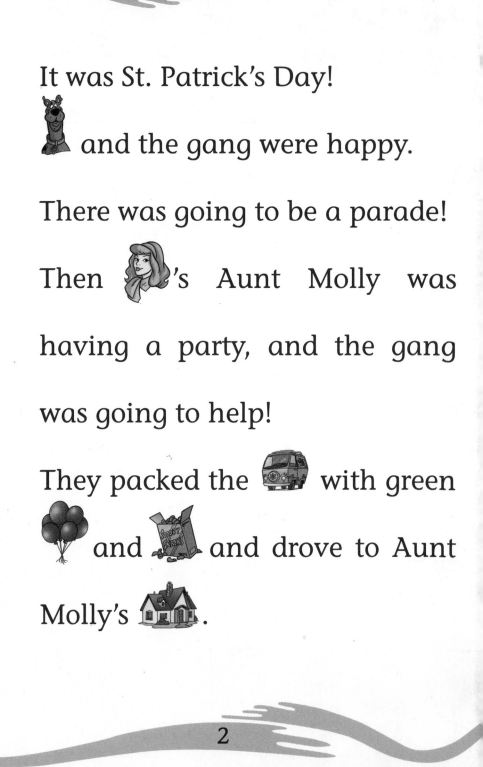 and drove to Aunt Molly's 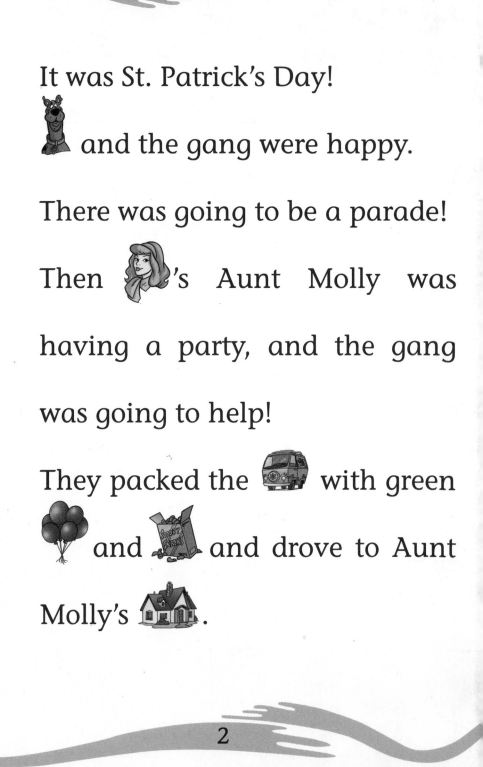.

There was a lot to do before the party.

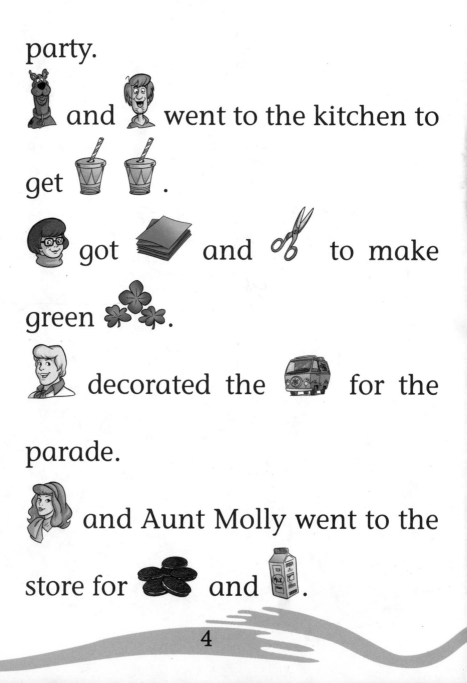 and went to the kitchen to get .

got and to make green .

decorated the for the parade.

and Aunt Molly went to the store for and .

Suddenly  and  shouted.

 and  ran to the kitchen.

"What's wrong?" asked .

 and  were shaking!

"Like, we saw a scary !" said

. "He had orange , a green

, and green !"

"Don't be silly," said . "A  is not scary!"

"This one was!" said .

"Where did the  go?" asked .

"Like, he ran out the back !" said .

"Let's look for him," said .

"No way," said .

 and  ran out of the kitchen.

But when  went back to her 🍀, they were gone!

"Jinkies!" she cried. "Someone stole the 🍀!"

"Ruh-roh!" said 🐕, and he hid under the 🪑.

"See?" said 🧑. "It was the 🧑!"

🧑 hid under the 🪑 with 🐕.

"Why are you under the 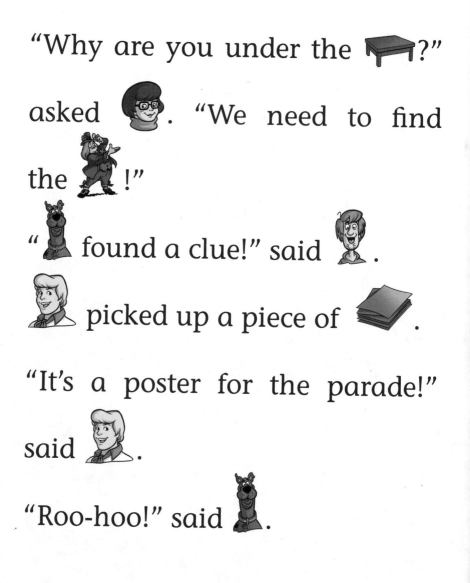?"
asked . "We need to find

the !"

" found a clue!" said .

picked up a piece of .

"It's a poster for the parade!"
said .

"Roo-hoo!" said .

drove the ⬛ in the parade.

"Keep your 👁 open!" he said.

"We have to find that 🧙 !"

🐕 , 🧑 , and 👩 waved out the ⬜ .

"Ruh-roh!" said 🐕 . He pointed

to a 🎪 with green ☘☘ .

Riding on the 🎪 was the 🧙 .

"Zoinks!" cried 🧑 .

🧑 and 🐕 hid in the back of the

🚐 .

"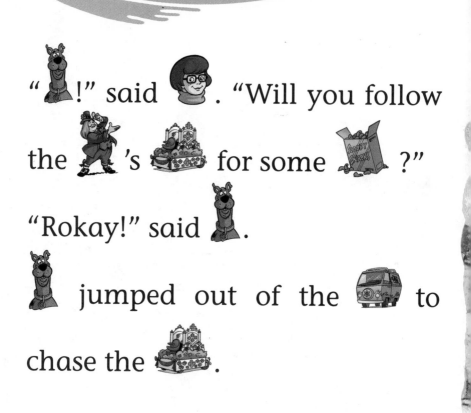!" said . "Will you follow

the 's for some ?"

"Rokay!" said .

 jumped out of the to

chase the .

When the  reached the finish line, was there.

He was standing with the !

"Hey, you!" said . "Are those our ? Did you take them from Aunt Molly's ?"

Just then, and Aunt Molly

arrived at the scene.

"What's going on?" asked .

 and 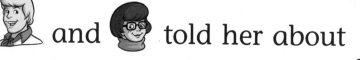 told her about

the missing and the .

"Oh, no!" laughed.

Aunt Molly walked up to the

 and pulled his orange .

It was a wig!

"That's no !" said . "This is my Uncle Sean!"

"I thought I'd borrow the ," said Uncle Sean, "and return them for the party!"

"Let's go to the party!" said .

"Let's eat!" said .

 ate some .

"Scooby-Dooby-Doo!"

Did you spot all the picture clues in this Scooby-Doo mystery?

Each picture clue is on a flash card. Ask a grown-up to cut out the flash cards. Then try reading the words on the back of the cards. The pictures will be your clue.

Reading is fun with Scooby-Doo!

Shaggy	Scooby
Velma	Daphne
Scooby Snacks	Fred

balloons	van
cup	house
scissors	paper

cookies	shamrocks
clothes	leprechaun
hat	hair

door	milk
eyes	table
float	window